Usborne Dinosaur Tales

The Dinosaur
With The Noisy SNORE

Russell Punter

Illustrated by Andy Elkerton

Reading consultant: Alison Kelly

Come and meet the
dinosaurs who live in
Dino Valley.

Look –
here's Sid...

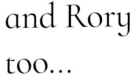

and Rory
too...

plus Molly...

Spike...

and Sally.

This story starts
at bedtime.

"I'm tired out,"
Sid sighs.

He snuggles down
beneath the sheets and
shuts his sleepy eyes.

Soon Sid's dreaming
sweetly. But just then,
from next door,

there comes a rumbling,
grumbling sound...

6

a loud, ear-splitting

SNORE!

"What a dreadful noise,"
says Sid. "I can't sleep
with that snore."

He storms around to Rory's house and knocks hard on his door.

Rory staggers to the door.

"Please quieten down,"
Sid begs.

"Yeah, whatever,"
Rory yawns.

Sid shuffles back to bed.

Sid gets home and tries to sleep. But then, just like before,

there comes a rumbling, grumbling sound...

a shaking, quaking

SNORE!

"Oh no, not again!"
Sid moans.

He marches off next door.

The noise has woken Sid's
three friends.

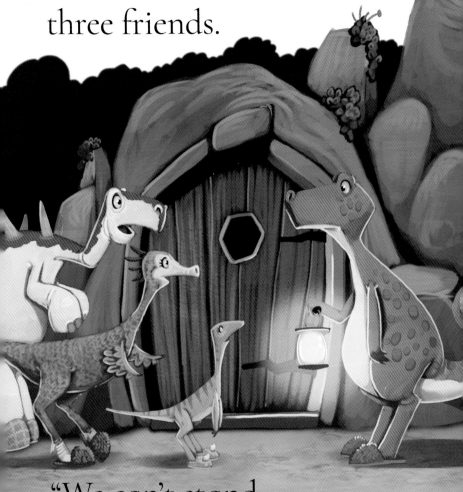

"We can't stand
Rory's snore!"

Knocking doesn't
work at all.

The friends are
forced to shout.

16

"Please stop snoring!" they all yell.

Soon Rory's head pokes out.

"Buy some ear plugs!"
Rory booms.

"That's just not fair,"
says Sally.

"Think of others,"
Molly begs.

"You're being mean,"
adds Spike.

20

Rory feels bad
when they have gone.

Perhaps his friends
are right?

He trudges off into the
night, in search of an idea.

Look, there's a hut, far
from his friends.

22

"They won't hear me
out here!"

He lumbers in and
falls asleep.

The long dark night
ticks by.

They climb inside to take the food.

There's lots to steal, for sure.

26

Then comes a rumbling, grumbling sound...

a huge, earth-trembling...

"What was that?" one raptor croaks.

"Perhaps a monster's near?"

"It sounds ginormous!"
wails his friend.

"Let's all get out of here!"

The three run screaming past Sid's house.

There's panic in their eyes.

Sid wakes up and looks outside.

"What's going on?" he cries.

"We'll leave the food that's in your hut!"

"Your monster's fierce," they shout.

"What's that? What monster?" wonders Sid.

He goes to check it out.

He takes the path down
to the hut, and opens up
the door.

There comes a rumbling,
grumbling sound...

a loud, familiar

SNORE!

When the new day comes around, Sid gives his friend a shake.

"Oh no," says Rory,
"not again! Did I keep
you awake?"

"No, you saved our food," says Sid. He tells his friend the story.

Now a new sign's
on the hut.

DINOSAUR VALLEY
WINTER FOOD STORE

BEWARE
OF THE
MONSTER!

"What monster?"
wonders Rory.

41

"You're the monster,"
Sid replies.

"Please sleep here
every night.

Your snore will scare off
any thieves.

They're sure to get
a fright."

"And look – we've bought a bed for you!"

That night,
just like before...

Rory falls asleep, and then,
he gives a massive...

Series editor: Lesley Sims

DINOSAUR VALLEY
WINTER FOOD STORE

BEWARE
OF THE
MONSTER!

THIEVES
KEEP OUT!

First published in 2021 by Usborne Publishing Ltd., Usborne House,
83-85 Saffron Hill, London EC1N 8RT, England. usborne.com
Copyright © 2021 Usborne Publishing Ltd.

USBORNE FIRST READING
Level Four

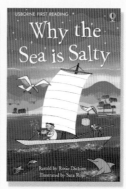

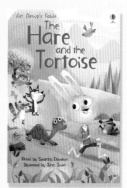

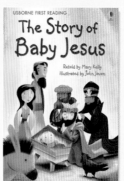

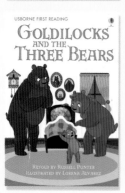

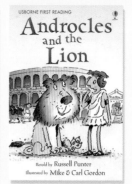

USBORNE FIRST READING
Level Three

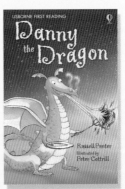

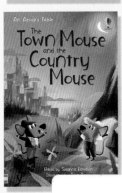

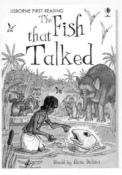